Disney
CLUB PENGUIN™

What Your Puffle Says About You

by Katherine Noll

Grosset & Dunlap
An Imprint of Penguin Group (USA) Inc.

GROSSET & DUNLAP
Published by the Penguin Group
Penguin Group (USA) Inc., 375 Hudson Street, New York, New York 10014, USA
Penguin Group (Canada), 90 Eglinton Avenue East, Suite 700, Toronto, Ontario M4P 2Y3, Canada
(a division of Pearson Penguin Canada Inc.)
Penguin Books Ltd., 80 Strand, London WC2R 0RL, England
Penguin Group Ireland, 25 St. Stephen's Green, Dublin 2, Ireland (a division of Penguin Books Ltd.)
Penguin Group (Australia), 250 Camberwell Road, Camberwell, Victoria 3124, Australia
(a division of Pearson Australia Group Pty. Ltd.)
Penguin Books India Pvt. Ltd., 11 Community Centre, Panchsheel Park, New Delhi—110 017, India
Penguin Group (NZ), 67 Apollo Drive, Rosedale, North Shore 0632, New Zealand
(a division of Pearson New Zealand Ltd.)
Penguin Books (South Africa) (Pty.) Ltd., 24 Sturdee Avenue, Rosebank, Johannesburg 2196, South Africa

Penguin Books Ltd., Registered Offices: 80 Strand, London WC2R 0RL, England

© 2011 Disney. All rights reserved. Used under license by Penguin Young Readers Group. Published by
Grosset & Dunlap, a division of Penguin Young Readers Group, 345 Hudson Street, New York, New York
10014. GROSSET & DUNLAP is a trademark of Penguin Group (USA) Inc. Printed in the U.S.A.

ISBN 978-0-448-45538-9   10 9 8 7 6 5 4 3 2 1

Welcome, puffle fan! As you may know, puffles are friendly, adorable creatures, and each has its own unique talents. But do you know which puffle you are most like? Or what that says about your personality? Grab a pen and get ready to find out!

Answer everything honestly and you'll be paired with the puffle who is most like you. Then let your imagination run wild as you design outfits based on your puffle color, dream up a unique puffle vacation, and create the coolest puffle party ever.

Ready for your puffle journey to begin? Turn the page and get started!

All About Me!

There is only one you! So before you find out which puffle you're most like, share a little bit about what makes you YOU.

I was born on _20 18_. I am _6_ years old.

My favorite flavor of birthday cake is _choclit_.

My school is called _hawerb_ and

I'm in _1_ grade.

Glue a photo or picture you have drawn of yourself here.

The best teacher I've ever had is _MRS. berger p is r i m a hab_. My favorite subject is _owt sib_. My least favorite subject is _math_.

These are the names of the people in my family: _gage_.

We live in _Hawerd_. I help out around the house

by _laeting the beg_. If my family and I could go

anywhere for vacation, I would pick _the left_.

These are some of my all-time favorite fun things:

Movie: mareo

Television Show: sonic

Game: sonic manea

Actor/Actress:

Book: bog man

Singer/Band: a magen brag

Song: BLever

Color: YeLowe

When it's breakfast time, I want to chow down on sereL.

My favorite meal for lunch is hot bogs and for dinner

is ~~hot snack~~ chicen. I love to snack on Froot snack.

If I could choose between staying up late or waking up early, I

would choose to sleep.

My favorite day of the week is sater bay because

i get to eat besf.t

My favorite season is winter. The holiday I most look

forward to every year is cristmis.

More About Me!

My penguin name is

senthev.

When I'm on Club Penguin, you'll most

likely find me hanging out at (the)

meting.

The first pin I ever found was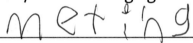

bahsing.

You'll always see me wearing

santhing.

A stage character I most want to be is

_____.

The Club Penguin job I would like is

_____.

My favorite Club Penguin game is _____,

but I'm also really good at _____

and _____.

If I could meet any Club Penguin character, it

would be _____.

The coolest Club Penguin party I ever went to

was _____.

Which Puffle Are You?

Now that we know all the things that make you YOU, let's find out which puffle you are most like. Read each question and pick the answer that most matches how you feel or what you would do.

1. Your friend has just given you a gift for your birthday. You're hoping it's:

- A. a stuffed animal
- B. a treasure map
- C. a jump rope
- D. a cool hoodie
- E. a DVD of your favorite funny movie
- F. a CD of the latest hit songs
- G. paints, markers, and paper
- H. a matching hat, scarf, and mittens
- I. a whoopee cushion

2. It's snack time! You reach for:

- A. cookies and milk
- B. trail mix
- C. an apple or carrot sticks
- D. chips
- E. jelly beans
- F. chocolate
- G. cheese and crackers
- H. an ice pop
- I. gummy worms

3. It's time to go to school, and you get to pick your dream vehicle to get you there. You choose a/an:

A. party bus big enough to fit all your friends
B. pirate ship
C. racing bicycle
D. skateboard
E. hot air balloon
F. limousine
G. horse and carriage
H. snowmobile
I. elephant

4. Your school is adding a new class—and you get to pick what it is. You'd like to learn more about:

A. video games
B. bungee-jumping
C. gymnastics
D. skateboarding
E. juggling
F. dancing
G. movie-making
H. ice-skating
I. how to make balloon animals

5. What word would you say best describes you?

A. loyal
B. adventurous
C. athletic
D. cool
E. funny
F. diva
G. artistic
H. shy
(I.) silly

6. Which of the following traits do you like LEAST in other people?

A. bossy
B. fearful
C. lazy
D. sweet
E. serious
F. messy
G. critical
(H.) noisy
I. boring

7. Two of your good friends are having an argument. What do you do?

(A.) Stay calm and try to help them work things out.
B. Have them settle the dispute by arm-wrestling.
C. Suggest they go for a brisk walk or run to blow off some steam.
D. Roll your eyes.
E. Do or say something to make them laugh.
F. Tell them to knock it off or you're out of there!
G. Get them to write a poem about how they feel.
H. Hide—you can't stand too much drama.
I. You are so busy running around and playing, you haven't even noticed they are fighting.

8. You are eating dinner at a friend's house. A plate of strange-looking food is placed in front of you. You:

A. Try to be polite and take a taste.
B. Dig right in—you're not afraid to try new things.
C. Ask what it is—you want to make sure it's something healthy.
D. Grab a snack from your backpack and eat that instead.
E. Distract everyone from the fact that you're not eating by telling a joke.
F. Ask if they can make you something else.
G. Play with your food and turn it into an artistic masterpiece.
H. Hide it in your napkin when no one is looking.
I. Devour the entire plate and ask for more.

9. Your favorite color is:

A. blue
B. red
C. pink
D. black
E. green
F. purple
G. yellow
H. white
I. orange

Answers

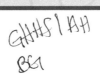

 If you chose **mostly As,**
you are most like a loyal and friendly blue puffle.

 If you chose **mostly Bs,**
you are most like an adventurous and fearless red puffle.

 If you chose **mostly Cs,**
you are most like a sporty and cheery pink puffle.

 If you chose **mostly Ds,**
you are most like a strong and silent **black** puffle.

 If you chose **mostly Es,**
you are most like a playful and silly green puffle.

 If you chose **mostly Fs,**
you are most like an elegant and picky **purple** puffle.

 If you chose **mostly Gs,**
you are most like an artistic and creative yellow puffle.

 If you chose **mostly Hs,**
you are most like a gentle and shy white puffle.

 If you chose **mostly Is,**
you are most like a zany and hyper orange puffle.

If you tied between two letters, pick which color you like better. That's your answer!

Did you find you're not exactly like just one puffle? Spend some time finding out how much you have in common with each of the nine different puffle types on the following pages.

True Blue

Just like a blue puffle, you are friendly and easygoing. Whether your friends want to go to the movies or chill out at home, it's all good with you. You get along with mostly everyone and are happiest when you are hanging out with your friends at home.

How Much Like a Blue Puffle Are You?

Find out how much you have in common with a blue puffle. Read the following statements and then pick how well they describe you on a scale of 1 to 10. 1 means the statement does not describe you at all, 5 means it describes you somewhat, and 10 means it describes you perfectly. Circle the number that best matches how you feel.

My favorite place to hang out on Club Penguin is my igloo.

| 1 | 2 | 3 | 4 | 5 | 6 | 7 | 8 | 9 | 10 |

I am pretty calm and don't get mad very often.

| 1 | 2 | 3 | 4 | 5 | 6 | 7 | 8 | 9 | 10 |

One of my favorite toys is a ball.

| 1 | 2 | 3 | 4 | 5 | 6 | 7 | 8 | 9 | 10 |

My favorite Club Penguin mini-game is *Puffle Rescue*.

| 1 | 2 | 3 | 4 | 5 | 6 | 7 | 8 | 9 | 10 |

I don't like scary stories—it is hard for me to fall asleep after listening to them.

| 1 | 2 | 3 | 4 | 5 | 6 | 7 | 8 | 9 | 10 |

My favorite Club Penguin play is *The Penguins That Time Forgot*.

| 1 | 2 | 3 | 4 | 5 | 6 | 7 | 8 | 9 | 10 |

My friends would describe me as very loyal.

| 1 | 2 | 3 | 4 | 5 | 6 | 7 | 8 | 9 | 10 |

I don't get bored often—I can usually find something fun to do.

| 1 | 2 | 3 | 4 | 5 | 6 | 7 | 8 | 9 | 10 |

If my friends have a problem, they normally ask me for help.

| 1 | 2 | 3 | 4 | 5 | 6 | 7 | 8 | 9 | 10 |

I enjoy making new friends and meeting new people.

| 1 | 2 | 3 | 4 | 5 | 6 | 7 | 8 | 9 | 10 |

Now add up all of your circled answers to find out how blue you are!

I am _____ percent blue!

Adventure Awaits!

Life is never dull with you around. Just like a red puffle, you are always in search of adventure. When your friends are bored, they know you'll turn up the excitement!

How Much Like a Red Puffle Are You?

Find out how much you have in common with a red puffle. Read the following statements and then pick how well they describe you on a scale of 1 to 10.

I am not afraid to try new things.

| 1 | 2 | 3 | 4 | 5 | 6 | 7 | 8 | 9 | 10 |

My favorite place to hang out on Club Penguin is the Cove.

| 1 | 2 | 3 | 4 | 5 | 6 | 7 | 8 | 9 | 10 |

One of my favorite sports is bowling.

| 1 | 2 | 3 | 4 | 5 | 6 | 7 | 8 | 9 | 10 |

My friends would describe me as adventurous.

| 1 | 2 | 3 | 4 | 5 | 6 | 7 | 8 | 9 | 10 |

My favorite Club Penguin mini-game is *Catchin' Waves*.

| 1 | 2 | 3 | 4 | 5 | 6 | 7 | 8 | 9 | 10 |

I don't like sleeping late.

| 1 | 2 | 3 | 4 | 5 | 6 | 7 | 8 | 9 | 10 |

I would love to have the chance to go skydiving or bungee jumping one day.

| 1 | 2 | 3 | 4 | 5 | 6 | 7 | 8 | 9 | 10 |

My favorite Club Penguin play is *Quest for the Golden Puffle*.

| 1 | 2 | 3 | 4 | 5 | 6 | 7 | 8 | 9 | 10 |

It is hard for me to sit still.

| 1 | 2 | 3 | 4 | 5 | 6 | 7 | 8 | 9 | 10 |

I know how to surf or I would like to learn one day.

| 1 | 2 | 3 | 4 | 5 | 6 | 7 | 8 | 9 | 10 |

Now add up all of your circled answers to find out how red you are!

I am _____ percent red!

Go for the Gold

When recess rolls around, your friends always know they can find you organizing a game of ball or tag. Just like a pink puffle, you are very athletic. You're a good sport, and you always have a smile on your face, win or lose.

How Much Like a Pink Puffle Are You?

Find out how much you have in common with a pink puffle. Read the following statements and then pick how well they describe you on a scale of 1 to 10.

My favorite place to hang out on Club Penguin is the Ice Rink.

| 1 | 2 | 3 | 4 | 5 | 6 | 7 | 8 | 9 | 10 |

I'd rather watch a football game than a cartoon.

| 1 | 2 | 3 | 4 | 5 | 6 | 7 | 8 | 9 | 10 |

One of my favorite toys is a jump rope.

| 1 | 2 | 3 | 4 | 5 | 6 | 7 | 8 | 9 | 10 |

I don't eat a lot of junk food.

| 1 | 2 | 3 | 4 | 5 | 6 | 7 | 8 | 9 | 10 |

My favorite Club Penguin mini-game is *Aqua Grabber*.

| 1 | 2 | 3 | 4 | 5 | 6 | 7 | 8 | 9 | 10 |

My friends would describe me as very active.

| 1 | 2 | 3 | 4 | 5 | 6 | 7 | 8 | 9 | 10 |

I play on at least one sports team.

| 1 | 2 | 3 | 4 | 5 | 6 | 7 | 8 | 9 | 10 |

I dislike rainy days because they mean I won't be able to go outside and play.

| 1 | 2 | 3 | 4 | 5 | 6 | 7 | 8 | 9 | 10 |

My favorite Club Penguin play is *Team Blue's Rally Debut*.

| 1 | 2 | 3 | 4 | 5 | 6 | 7 | 8 | 9 | 10 |

I like to keep my room clean.

| 1 | 2 | 3 | 4 | 5 | 6 | 7 | 8 | 9 | 10 |

Now add up all of your circled answers to find out how pink you are!

I am _____ percent pink!

Keeping it Cool

Just like a black puffle, you like to keep people guessing about how you feel. Are you happy, angry, or sad? No one knows for sure, because you aren't very talkative. It's not because you're shy, you just prefer to keep things to yourself.

How Much Like a Black Puffle Are You?

Find out how much you have in common with a black puffle. Read the following statements and then pick how well they describe you on a scale of 1 to 10.

My favorite place to hang out on Club Penguin is the Underground Pool.

| 1 | 2 | 3 | 4 | 5 | 6 | 7 | 8 | 9 | 10 |

It's important for me to have time where I can be by myself.

| 1 | 2 | 3 | 4 | 5 | 6 | 7 | 8 | 9 | 10 |

One of my most prized possessions is my skateboard.

| 1 | 2 | 3 | 4 | 5 | 6 | 7 | 8 | 9 | 10 |

My favorite Club Penguin mini-game is *Cart Surfer*.

| 1 | 2 | 3 | 4 | 5 | 6 | 7 | 8 | 9 | 10 |

You would never catch me wearing anything pink.

| 1 | 2 | 3 | 4 | 5 | 6 | 7 | 8 | 9 | 10 |

My friends would describe me as the strong and silent type.

| 1 | 2 | 3 | 4 | 5 | 6 | 7 | 8 | 9 | 10 |

I don't like following rules. I prefer to do my own thing.

| 1 | 2 | 3 | 4 | 5 | 6 | 7 | 8 | 9 | 10 |

I like fiery, hot foods.

| 1 | 2 | 3 | 4 | 5 | 6 | 7 | 8 | 9 | 10 |

My favorite Club Penguin play is *Ruby and the Ruby*.

| 1 | 2 | 3 | 4 | 5 | 6 | 7 | 8 | 9 | 10 |

I dislike big crowds.

| 1 | 2 | 3 | 4 | 5 | 6 | 7 | 8 | 9 | 10 |

Now add up all of your circled answers to find out how black you are!

I am _____ percent black!

Giggles Galore

What's life without some laughs? Your friends can always count on you to make them chuckle, and you're happy to do it. Just like a green puffle, you like to spread the fun around!

How Much Like a Green Puffle Are You?

Find out how much you have in common with a green puffle. Read the following statements and then pick how well they describe you on a scale of 1 to 10.

My favorite place to hang out on Club Penguin is the Lighthouse.

| 1 | 2 | 3 | 4 | 5 | 6 | 7 | 8 | 9 | 10 |

I have a lot of energy.

| 1 | 2 | 3 | 4 | 5 | 6 | 7 | 8 | 9 | 10 |

I would love to learn how to ride a unicycle.

| 1 | 2 | 3 | 4 | 5 | 6 | 7 | 8 | 9 | 10 |

I get bored very easily.

| 1 | 2 | 3 | 4 | 5 | 6 | 7 | 8 | 9 | 10 |

My favorite Club Penguin mini-game is *Jet Pack Adventure*.

| 1 | 2 | 3 | 4 | 5 | 6 | 7 | 8 | 9 | 10 |

My friends would describe me as silly.

| 1 | 2 | 3 | 4 | 5 | 6 | 7 | 8 | 9 | 10 |

I really enjoy making other people laugh.

| 1 | 2 | 3 | 4 | 5 | 6 | 7 | 8 | 9 | 10 |

Sometimes I get in trouble for clowning around.

| 1 | 2 | 3 | 4 | 5 | 6 | 7 | 8 | 9 | 10 |

My favorite Club Penguin play is *Fairy Fables*.

| 1 | 2 | 3 | 4 | 5 | 6 | 7 | 8 | 9 | 10 |

I like being the center of attention.

| 1 | 2 | 3 | 4 | 5 | 6 | 7 | 8 | 9 | 10 |

Now add up all of your circled answers to find out how green you are!

I am _____ percent green!

Dancing Diva

Just like a purple puffle, you enjoy the finer things in life. You're picky about what you wear and what you eat. But the one thing you are not at all fussy about is dancing. You'll bust a move anytime, anywhere.

How Much Like a Purple Puffle Are You?

Find out how much you have in common with a purple puffle. Read the following statements and then pick how well they describe you on a scale of 1 to 10.

My favorite place to hang out on Club Penguin is the Night Club.

| 1 | 2 | 3 | 4 | 5 | 6 | 7 | 8 | 9 | 10 |

I spend a lot of time choosing what I'm going to wear each day.

| 1 | 2 | 3 | 4 | 5 | 6 | 7 | 8 | 9 | 10 |

I like blowing bubbles.

| 1 | 2 | 3 | 4 | 5 | 6 | 7 | 8 | 9 | 10 |

I don't like getting dirty.

| 1 | 2 | 3 | 4 | 5 | 6 | 7 | 8 | 9 | 10 |

My favorite Club Penguin mini-game is *Dance Contest*.

(1   2   3   4   5   6   7   8   9   10)

My friends would describe me as a bit of a princess/prince, and I agree!

(1   2   3   4   5   6   7   8   9   10)

I love to dance.

(1   2   3   4   5   6   7   8   9   10)

I usually complain about what's for dinner.

(1   2   3   4   5   6   7   8   9   10)

My favorite Club Penguin play is *The Haunting of the Viking Opera*.

(1   2   3   4   5   6   7   8   9   10)

I always remember to say "please" and "thank you."

(1   2   3   4   5   6   7   8   9   10)

Now add up all of your circled answers to find out how purple you are!

I am _____ percent purple!

A Creative Dreamer

 A dreamer like you always has your head in the clouds. Even if it seems like you're not paying attention to the busy world around you, you're just getting inspiration for your next project, which could be anything from a painting to a poem. Just like a yellow puffle, you are a true artist.

How Much Like a Yellow Puffle Are You?

Find out how much you have in common with a yellow puffle. Read the following statements and then pick how well they describe you on a scale of 1 to 10.

My favorite place to hang out on Club Penguin is the Stage.

| 1 | 2 | 3 | 4 | 5 | 6 | 7 | 8 | 9 | 10 |

I enjoy writing short stories and poems.

| 1 | 2 | 3 | 4 | 5 | 6 | 7 | 8 | 9 | 10 |

My most prized possessions are the pieces of art I have created.

| 1 | 2 | 3 | 4 | 5 | 6 | 7 | 8 | 9 | 10 |

I find myself daydreaming a lot.

| 1 | 2 | 3 | 4 | 5 | 6 | 7 | 8 | 9 | 10 |

My favorite Club Penguin mini-game is mixing music in *DJ3K*.

| 1 | 2 | 3 | 4 | 5 | 6 | 7 | 8 | 9 | 10 |

My friends would describe me as artistic.

| 1 | 2 | 3 | 4 | 5 | 6 | 7 | 8 | 9 | 10 |

I'm not really into sports.

| 1 | 2 | 3 | 4 | 5 | 6 | 7 | 8 | 9 | 10 |

My friends and family ask me to draw pictures for them.

| 1 | 2 | 3 | 4 | 5 | 6 | 7 | 8 | 9 | 10 |

My favorite Club Penguin play is *Underwater Adventure*.

| 1 | 2 | 3 | 4 | 5 | 6 | 7 | 8 | 9 | 10 |

I would definitely try out for the school play.

| 1 | 2 | 3 | 4 | 5 | 6 | 7 | 8 | 9 | 10 |

Now add up all of your circled answers to find out how yellow you are!

I am _____ percent yellow!

Shy Yet Strong

Just like a white puffle, you are shy. But your friends know that you have an inner strength and will turn to you for help whenever they have a problem. You also love the cold weather and everything that comes with it.

How Much Like a White Puffle Are You?

Find out how much you have in common with a white puffle. Read the following statements and then pick how well they describe you on a scale of 1 to 10.

My favorite place to hang out on Club Penguin is the Dojo.

| 1 | 2 | 3 | 4 | 5 | 6 | 7 | 8 | 9 | 10 |

I don't like a lot of noise.

| (1) | 2 | 3 | 4 | 5 | 6 | 7 | 8 | 9 | 10 |

My favorite season is winter.

| 1 | 2 | 3 | 4 | 5 | 6 | 7 | 8 | 9 | (10) |

If I see a friend in need, I always try and help them.

| 1 | 2 | 3 | 4 | 5 | 6 | 7 | 8 | 9 | (10) |

My favorite Club Penguin mini-game is *Card-Jitsu*.

| 1 | 2 | 3 | 4 | 5 | 6 | 7 | 8 | 9 | 10 |

I love it when there's a snow day.

| 1 | 2 | 3 | 4 | 5 | 6 | 7 | 8 | 9 | (10) |

My friends would describe me as gentle.

| 1 | 2 | 3 | 4 | 5 | 6 | 7 | 8 | 9 | (10) |

My favorite activity is ice-skating.

| (1) | 2 | 3 | 4 | 5 | 6 | 7 | 8 | 9 | 10 |

The idea of getting up and speaking in front of a room full of people scares me.

| (1) | 2 | 3 | 4 | 5 | 6 | 7 | 8 | 9 | 10 |

My favorite Club Penguin play is *Secrets of the Bamboo Forest*.

| 1 | 2 | 3 | 4 | 5 | 6 | 7 | 8 | 9 | 10 |

Now add up all of your circled answers to find out how white you are!

I am _____ percent white!

Off-the-Wall

Everyone knows when you're around. You're impossible to ignore! Just like an orange puffle, your off-the-wall antics get you noticed. Your zany, high-energy personality makes everyone wonder what you'll do next.

How Much Like an Orange Puffle Are You?

Find out how much you have in common with an orange puffle. Read the following statements and then pick how well they describe you on a scale of 1 to 10.

You'll find me on Club Penguin wherever there's the biggest crowd of penguins.

| 1 | 2 | 3 | 4 | 5 | 6 | 7 | 8 | 9 | 10 |

I almost always have a smile on my face.

| 1 | 2 | 3 | 4 | 5 | 6 | 7 | 8 | 9 | 10 |

I am not fussy about food and will eat just about anything.

| 1 | 2 | 3 | 4 | 5 | 6 | 7 | 8 | 9 | 10 |

One of my favorite toys is a hula hoop.

| 1 | 2 | 3 | 4 | 5 | 6 | 7 | 8 | 9 | 10 |

My favorite Club Penguin mini-game is *Pizzatron 3000*.

| 1 | 2 | 3 | 4 | 5 | 6 | 7 | 8 | 9 | 10 |

Most people I know have a hard time keeping up with me.

| 1 | 2 | 3 | 4 | 5 | 6 | 7 | 8 | 9 | 10 |

My friends would describe me as zany.

| 1 | 2 | 3 | 4 | 5 | 6 | 7 | 8 | 9 | 10 |

Not everyone gets my sense of humor.

| 1 | 2 | 3 | 4 | 5 | 6 | 7 | 8 | 9 | 10 |

My favorite Club Penguin play is *Norman Swarm Has Been Transformed*.

| 1 | 2 | 3 | 4 | 5 | 6 | 7 | 8 | 9 | 10 |

Sometimes people tell me I talk too much.

| 1 | 2 | 3 | 4 | 5 | 6 | 7 | 8 | 9 | 10 |

Now add up all of your circled answers to find out how orange you are!

I am _____ percent orange!

A Friend for Everyone

Did you discover you are most like an orange puffle, but you already own a purple puffle? Does this mean you won't get along with your puffle pet? Don't panic! Puffles bring out the best in others.

Blue Puffle

Easygoing blue-types are up for anything, whether it's a treasure hunt with a red friend, watching a funny movie with a green, or building a snowman with white-types.

Red Puffle

Fearless red-types are full of excitement and can help bring out the sense of adventure in timid white-types and picky purple-types.

Pink Puffle

Athletic pink-types inspire their friends to get moving and are particularly good at getting more indoor-types like yellows and blues outside for some fun.

Black Puffle

Cool and collected black-types may enjoy their alone time, but have a calming influence on their friends, especially hyper orange.

Green Puffle

Green-types can make their friends laugh with ease, but have a knack for helping focused pink-types and dreamy yellows see the sillier side of life.

Purple Puffle

Posh purple-types influence all of their friends to be more elegant, and persuade silly greens, zany oranges, and reckless red-types to mind their manners.

Yellow Puffle

Artistic yellow-types see the world in a different way, and they help their friends see things differently, too. Creative yellows can help quiet black-types express themselves.

White Puffle

Sweet and gentle white-types remind all of their friends to be kinder. They are also good at reminding energetic reds and active pinks to relax.

Orange Puffle

Quirky orange-types march to the beat of their own drummers and don't mind looking foolish. Their antics can make even serious black-types and proper purples giggle.

All About My Friends

If a movie was made about our friendship, the title would be

_____.

When my friends and I get together, we love to

_____.

I couldn't imagine life without my best pals. They are:

_____

_____

_____

_____

If my friends were animals, they would be:

_____

_____

_____

_____

If you took all of our favorite foods and made a pizza out of them, you'd have a
_____ pizza.

My friends and I have to get up and dance when we hear this song:
_____.

If we made a flag to celebrate our friendship,

it would have this symbol on it: _____

and these colors: _____.

If I mixed my puffle's color with my friends' puffles' colors, I'd get these colors:

_____

_____

_____

_____

_____

Draw your friendship flag here.

My Friends' and Family's Puffle Personalities

Blue

My friends who are most like blue puffles are:

_____

My family members who are most like blue puffles are:

_____

My teachers and classmates who are most like blue puffles are:

_____

Red

My friends who are most like red puffles are:

_____

My family members who are most like red puffles are:

_____

My teachers and classmates who are most like red puffles are:

_____

Pink

My friends who are most like pink puffles are:

_____

My family members who are most like pink puffles are:

_____

My teachers and classmates who are most like pink puffles are:

_____

Black

My friends who are most like black puffles are:

_____

My family members who are most like black puffles are:

_____

My teachers and classmates who are most like black puffles are:

_____

Green

My friends who are most like green puffles are:

_____

My family members who are most like green puffles are:

_____

My teachers and classmates who are most like green puffles are:

_____

Purple

My friends who are most like purple puffles are:

_____

My family members who are most like purple puffles are:

_____

My teachers and classmates who are most like purple puffles are:

_____

Yellow

My friends who are most like yellow puffles are:

_____

My family members who are most like yellow puffles are:

_____

My teachers and classmates who are most like yellow puffles are:

_____

White

My friends who are most like white puffles are:

_____

My family members who are most like white puffles are:

_____

My teachers and classmates who are most like white puffles are:

_____

Orange

My friends who are most like orange puffles are:
_____

My family members who are most like orange puffles are:
_____

My teachers and classmates who are most like orange puffles are:
_____

A Puffle Vacation

Mix and match puffle personalities to create the most unique vacation ever! Circle your vacation choices in the story. You can even have a friend circle theirs in a different color so that you can compare results.

It's vacation time and you're headed to the beach/**a big city**/~~the mountains~~. You know you can't leave home without your favorite stuffed animal/**MP3 player**/book, so you make sure to pack it. You get on a/an boat/hot air balloon/**airplane** and begin your journey.

Once you've reached your destination, you check into your ~~cabin~~/bed-and-breakfast/**circus tent**. The first thing you want to do is visit a/an zoo/**amusement park**/museum. After you're done, you decide to do some souvenir shopping. You buy a **postcard**/T-shirt with a funny saying on it/baseball cap.

When you wake up the next day, the weather is beautiful and you decide to spend some time outdoors swimming/~~skiing~~/**skateboarding**. It makes you hungry so you stop for dinner at a/an **fancy restaurant**/ice cream parlor/salad bar.

After a fun, busy week, it's time to head home. You're sad to be leaving because you had such a good time, but you're happy to return because you want to tell your friends funny stories about your trip/**need some alone time**/were starting to feel homesick.

Now that you've created a one-of-a-kind puffle vacation, draw a scene from your adventures on this postcard:

What's Your Style?

What does your puffle personality say about your fashion style? Read more to find out, then mix and match puffle clothing items to come up with your own special outfit.

Blue Puffle

If you're most like a blue puffle, you have a classic, preppy style. You like to wear cardigan sweaters or polo shirts paired with blue jeans or skirts.

Red Puffle

If you're most like a red puffle, you have a more casual style. You like to wear comfortable clothing that you can move easily in, such as cargo pants and tank tops.

Pink Puffle

If you're most like a pink puffle, you have a sporty style. You like to wear jerseys or T-shirts of your favorite sports team paired with shorts or yoga pants.

Black Puffle

If you're most like a black puffle, you have a punk style. You like to wear skinny jeans and hoodies accessorized with studded belts and wristbands.

Green Puffle

If you're most like a green puffle, you have a bold style. You like to wear colorful clothing that has a lot of detail or a bright pattern.

Purple Puffle

If you're most like a purple puffle, you have a fashion-forward style. You like to wear the hottest fashions and accessorize with trendy purses and jewelry.

Yellow Puffle

If you're most like a yellow puffle, you have a cool Bohemian style. You like to wear artsy clothing such as long skirts, peasant tops, and scarves.

White Puffle

If you're most like a white puffle, you have a simple style. You like to wear pale, muted colors, jeans, hoodies, and unfussy accessories.

Orange Puffle

If you're most like an orange puffle, you have a zany style. You like to surprise people with your outfits, and you wear mismatched clothes and odd accessories to stand out.

It's Party Time!

Now that you know all about puffles, it's time to celebrate. Mix and match puffle personalities for a unique puffle party. Circle your party choices in the story.

You're throwing a party and you've decided to have a **dance party**/scavenger hunt/ **mystery party**. First you need to write out the invitations. You decide to invite all your family and friends/a few of your closest friends/your imaginary friends. On the invitation, you ask your guests to dress like a character from their favorite book/**dress like a superhero**/wear their clothes inside out.

You need to decorate for your guests. You **put whoopee cushions on all the chairs**/ blow up football-shaped balloons/**put a bouquet of flowers on all the tables**.

You also have to get the food ready. You're going to serve a fruit salad/**pizza**/ snow cones.

The guests have arrived and everyone is having a great time. For even more fun, you decide to organize some games for your guests. You have everyone do a craft activity/run relay races/**play musical chairs**.

The party's over and it's time for your guests to leave. You send everyone home with a goody bag filled with gag gifts/**a mix CD of your favorite songs**/candy.

My Puffles

Name of Puffle: _____

Color: _____

Date Adopted: _____

Likes: _____

Dislikes: _____

Name of Puffle: _____

Color: _____

Date Adopted: _____

Likes: _____

Dislikes: _____

Name of Puffle: _____

Color: _____

Date Adopted: _____

Likes: _____

Dislikes: _____

Name of Puffle: _____

Color: _____

Date Adopted: _____

Likes: _____

Dislikes: _____

Name of Puffle: _____

Color: _____

Date Adopted: _____

Likes: _____

Dislikes: _____

Name of Puffle: _____

Color: _____

Date Adopted: _____

Likes: _____

Dislikes: _____

Be on the lookout!

What kind of puffle would you like to see on Club Penguin?
Draw it below.

Name of Puffle: _____

Color: _____

Date Adopted: _____

Likes: _____

Dislikes: _____

Name of Puffle: _____

Color: _____

Date Adopted: _____

Likes: _____

Dislikes: _____

Name of Puffle: _____

Color: _____

Date Adopted: _____

Likes: _____

Dislikes: _____

Name of Puffle: _____

Color: _____

Date Adopted: _____

Likes: _____

Dislikes: _____

Name of Puffle: _____

Color: _____

Date Adopted: _____

Likes: _____

Dislikes: _____

Name of Puffle: _____

Color: _____

Date Adopted: _____

Likes: _____

Dislikes: _____